Beast Quest®

GLAKI
SPEAR OF THE DEPTHS

BY ADAM BLADE

ORCHARD

With special thanks to Tabitha Jones

www.beastquest.co.uk

ORCHARD BOOKS

First published in Great Britain in 2020 by The Watts Publishing Group

1 3 5 7 9 10 8 6 4 2

Text © Beast Quest Limited 2020
Cover and inside illustrations by Steve Sims
© Beast Quest Limited 2020

Beast Quest is a registered trademark of Beast Quest Limited
Series created by Beast Quest Limited, London

A CIP catalogue record for this book is available from the British Library.

ISBN 978 1 40836 188 7

Printed in Great Britain

The paper and board used in this book are made from wood from responsible sources

Orchard Books
An imprint of Hachette Children's Group
Part of The Watts Publishing Group Limited
Carmelite House, 50 Victoria Embankment, London EC4Y 0DZ

An Hachette UK Company
www.hachette.co.uk
www.hachettechildrens.co.uk

Welcome to the world of Beast Quest!

Tom was once an ordinary village boy, until he travelled to the City, met King Hugo and discovered his destiny. Now he is the Master of the Beasts, sworn to defend Avantia and its people against Evil. Tom draws on the might of the magical Golden Armour, and is protected by powerful tokens granted to him by the Good Beasts of Avantia. Together with his loyal companion Elenna, Tom is always ready to visit new lands and tackle the enemies of the realm.

While there's blood in his veins, Tom will never give up the Quest…

THE LABYRINTH JUNGLE

THE PEAKS OF DESPAIR

DANGER

DEATH

ZARGON'S
PRISON

HE MOAT OF
VAKUNDA

There are special gold coins to collect in this book. You will earn one coin for every chapter you read.

Find out what to do with your coins at the end of the book.

CONTENTS

When my aunt Aroha left Tangala to marry King Hugo of Avantia, I thought I could rule this kingdom. I wanted to make her proud, to protect the country's borders and keep my people safe.

I have failed. The sorcerer who took me claims to be hundreds of years old. He says he will not kill me, if my aunt does the right thing. It's the Jewels of Tangala that he wants. A simple swap – me for the magical stones. But if Aroha delivers them, the results will be far worse than one death. All Tangala will be in peril. My only hope is that my aunt has some other plan, some way to rescue me, but save the kingdom too.

She will need brave heroes at her side if she is to succeed.

Rotu
Regent of Tangala, and nephew to the queen.

THE LEGEND OF THE JEWELS

Tom and Elenna sat opposite Queen Aroha and Yara in the warm halo of light created by their campfire. The hills behind them echoed with the last calls of birds settling to roost, and the evening sky was a deep blue scattered with stars. The queen held the four Jewels of Tangala in one hand. She tilted them towards the flames so that rich flashes of colour shot through the polished gems. Yara, bodyguard to the queen's kidnapped nephew, Prince Rotu, gazed intently at the jewels. They all waited for Aroha to begin her tale.

Tom eased himself down to rest his elbow on his pack. After a good supper of dried meat he felt almost refreshed from their earlier battle against Lycaxa. The fearsome hound was the second Beast they had defeated on their Quest to rescue Rotu from Zargon. The Evil Wizard had demanded the jewels in exchange for the prince, so Tom was eager to find out more about the four magical gemstones.

Aroha's face was half hidden in flickering shadow, but her eyes shone as she met each of their gazes in turn before beginning her story.

"Once, many centuries ago, a Tangalan queen called Nala held a tournament to find herself a husband and consort, as was the custom in those days. It was a grand occasion, with much merrymaking, but not everyone was happy." The fire popped loudly. Aroha paused as a branch settled lower in the flames, then she went on.

"Unbeknownst to the queen, the Royal Goldsmith, Davron, had fallen

in love with her. Driven mad by
jealousy, he created a crown for the
new husband inlaid with jewels
that he had enchanted with a curse.
Though the consort had been a
good and honest man, the cursed
jewels made him hunger for power,

twisting his mind until he wanted the
kingdom for himself."

At Aroha's side, Yara nodded
vigorously. "He even tried to murder
the queen," she said, "but Nala's
maid stopped him. She was named
the queen's official bodyguard, as a

reward for her loyalty and bravery."

Aroha dipped her head. "That's right," she said. "On his arrest, the disgraced consort's crown was removed, and the curse was lifted from him. Horrified by what he had done, the poor man begged his queen for forgiveness. Nala began to suspect the jewels and confirmed her suspicions by trying on the crown herself. Having great wisdom and strength of character, the queen was able to resist the jewels' power, but she felt their pull enough to realise where the evil lay. She locked the jewels away, vowing that they would never see daylight again."

"It's a shame they didn't stay

hidden," Tom said. "How did Zargon get his hands on them?"

Aroha frowned down at the gleaming stones in her palm and let out a sigh. "Unfortunately, the jewels are so powerful that even under lock and key, they still call to those with evil in their hearts. Zargon was pulled to the magical gemstones. He stole them, and, as you know, created the Kingdom of Vakunda with its four Realms; jungle, mountains, river and palace – each with a Beast to protect them."

Tom gazed at the gemstones. Though the flames of their campfire had burned down to a smouldering glow, the jewels still pulsed with a light from within. "It's amazing to think that four small gems could create a whole kingdom!" he said.

"And then cause the very same kingdom to transform into a treacherous wasteland," Elenna added, pulling her cloak tighter about her. "It looks like they have the power to create and to destroy."

Aroha nodded. "When the four Jewels of Tangala were taken back from Zargon five hundred years ago, they sucked all the goodness out of Vakunda. This turned them into the perilous landscapes we have been crossing. Somehow, by vanquishing Zargon's Beasts, we are reversing that process."

Tom thought of how the treacherous jungle and the Peaks of Despair had changed after they had defeated the Beasts that guarded them. The jungle had become lush and beautiful, and the jagged mountain range had transformed into the gently rolling Hills of Plenty – but not before almost claiming their lives. The glowing embers of the fire spat out a shower of sparks, the flames now almost gone. Tom glanced about at the darkness pressing in on them and felt suddenly cold.

"We should get some rest," he said. "Tomorrow will be a long day."

Tom stretched himself out beside Elenna, using his pack as a pillow.

Aroha and Yara did the same, wrapping themselves in their travelling cloaks to keep out the chill of the night. But, as Tom tried to settle, a nagging unease kept prodding him awake. He couldn't help thinking of the strange, almost hungry light in Yara's eyes as she had watched the jewels in Aroha's hand. He turned to see Elenna still awake and alert too.

"Do you think we should keep a watch?" Elenna whispered. "I have a horrible feeling Yara's up to something."

Tom nodded. "I know what you mean. The way she keeps disappearing when we need her

most, and trying to get her hands on
the jewels... I'll take first watch,"
he said, though his eyes felt gritty
with exhaustion. He glanced across

at Yara, already snoring softly, then folded his arms on his chest.

Whatever you're up to, we'll get to the bottom of it.

Yara slept soundly through Tom's shift, and he swapped with Elenna halfway through the night. The next morning, he woke to a shadowy landscape wreathed in silver-grey mist, and Elenna's hand on his shoulder. "Did anything happen?" he asked her, pushing himself up to sitting.

Elenna grinned. "Apart from you snoring like a hog?" she said. Beyond the ashes of their fire, Yara shifted in her sleep, and Elenna's smile vanished. She shook her head. "She didn't stir. But I still think we should be wary."

After waking Yara and Aroha, Tom covered the remains of their fire with earth. With the sun a pale disc on the horizon, they set off into the hazy dawn.

The dewy grass that covered the lower slopes of the Hills of Plenty soon gave way to boggy marshland that squelched beneath their boots. Tendrils of mist twisted before them, like ghosts, drenching Tom so that he soon felt chilled to the bone.

The sun rose higher as they trudged onwards, but the fog around them only grew thicker, turning from milky white to yellow. A stench caught in Tom's throat, making his eyes burn.

Queen Aroha stopped and held up her map. "We will soon reach a ring-shaped inland lake, once called the Crystal Sea," she said. "Now it is known as the Moat of Vakunda. At its centre, we will find Zargon's prison."

The ground became more waterlogged still, sucking at Tom's feet with every step. The stink grew steadily worse until his head ached, and his throat felt raw. It felt like they had been walking all morning. Finally, the choking fog thinned. They all stopped dead in the sudden, watery sunlight, right at the edge of an enormous lake.

"The Crystal Sea," Elenna said, grimacing. Tom covered his nose,

almost gagging at the vile smell
rising from the water. A slimy scum
of greyish-green algae covered the
inland lake, and bubbles rose from
oozy mud near the water's edge,
popping to release more of the
stench. Wisps of sickly yellow vapour
drifted across the lake's surface.

The Sea of Slime, more like, Tom
thought.

"What kind of Beast could live
here?" Elenna asked, holding her
nose. "Something disgusting..."

"The legends speak of a creature
called Glaki, Spear of the Depths,"
Aroha said. "He is believed to guard
the lake, killing anyone who dares to
cross."

Gazing out over the rancid water, Tom tried to imagine how anything could possibly live in it. He tried not to shudder. If the ferocity of Zargon's last two Beasts was anything to go by, Glaki was sure to be a formidable enemy.

TREACHEROUS
WATERS

"Well, I definitely don't fancy swimming across," Elenna said, wrinkling her nose as she looked out over the filthy lake. "Let's see if we can find some driftwood and make a raft."

"Good idea," Tom said. After shooting Elenna a meaningful

glance, he turned to Queen Aroha. "How about you and Elenna head one way along the shore, and Yara and I go the other? That way, we've twice the chance of finding what we need. And it will give me a chance to get to know Yara better."

"That's fine with me," Aroha said. "But we should meet back here by noon."

Tom set off with Yara at his side, scanning the slick mud that edged the lake for any sign of driftwood. But apart from the occasional blackened stick, there wasn't much.

Yara chewed at her lip as they searched, as if lost in thought. *Time to find out more about her...*

"So, how long were you a bodyguard at the palace?" Tom asked.

Yara shot him a scornful look. "Longer than you've been alive," she said.

"It must have been difficult, guarding the regent," Tom said. "I've met Rotu, and he's not one to stay out of danger. How did he go missing?"

Yara flushed and clenched her jaw. "My failure will haunt me until the day I die," she said. "I believe Zargon must have slipped by me in the night, using some kind of magic. The prince went to bed as usual, and I guarded his chamber door. But when I went to wake him the next morning, his bed was empty. All that remained was the note you have seen, demanding the jewels."

"That must have been a terrible shock," Tom said, pulling a stick from the mud. It came free with a *pop*. It was too short to use, and Tom tossed it aside. "I am sure you must have mounted a search," he went on. "How do you think Zargon escaped the city? Rotu must have put up some kind of a fight."

Yara let out a huff of irritation. "There's no point in raking over the past," she said, stalking ahead of him. "I'm here now, willing to give my life to find Rotu if needed. I don't see why I should be lectured about my duty by a boy!"

Tom tried to think of something soothing to say. But before he could come up with anything, Yara pointed ahead towards a skeletal hulk of wood just visible through the mist.

"Isn't that a boat?" she said.

"You're right!" Tom said. They both broke into a jog, splashing over the boggy ground towards the stranded vessel. Tom thought they might salvage a few planks to make a raft. But, as they drew close, he saw that the boat was in good shape. The mast had broken so the top part hung crookedly, but the rest of the boat seemed intact. When he pressed

his boot against the blackened wood
of the hull, it felt sound – almost as
if the putrid water of the lake had
preserved the timber.

"Go and get the others!" Yara said.
"I'll check the boat for leaks." Tom

hesitated. *What if she disappears again?* But then he nodded, and turned to race back along the shore. *I need her to think that I trust her. For now, anyway.*

A short while later, Aroha and Elenna sat side by side at the bow of the dinghy. They each held an oar that Tom had made from the broken mast. Yara looked back at Tom from the stern as he gave the vessel a hefty shove out on to the water, then leapt aboard, taking his seat beside her.

Snaking coils of vapour rose from the water's surface, carrying with them the eye-watering stench of the lake. Tom pulled his tunic up to cover his nose, but the smell even seeped into his clothes. Aroha and Elenna paddled with strong, steady strokes, quickly carrying them out into open water. The lake's surface was eerily still. But every once in a while, something stirred below with a *plop*, sending out circles of ripples. Peering down through the film of oily scum that covered the water, Tom could make out nothing except murky shadows. His skin prickled with dread.

The jagged outlines of several small, rocky islands emerged from the low mist ahead. "We'd better give those a wide berth," Tom said, pointing. "There might be rocks beneath the surface." He angled the rudder at the back of the boat, setting a course between the islands. As they neared the first, Tom lurched sideways, the tiller pulling against his grip as the dinghy veered sharply towards land. It felt as if the boat was being drawn by a strong current. *What's going on?* This didn't feel right at all. Tom frowned, adjusting the tiller and trying to correct their path. The boat only picked up speed, swerving towards the rocks.

"Paddle harder or we'll run aground," Yara cried. Grunting with effort, Elenna and Aroha doubled

the speed of their strokes. *No use.* The
rudder strained against Tom's grip
and the island only drew closer. He
felt his heartbeat quicken as the rocks
towered over them. This wasn't right
at all. *What was…*

"A whirlpool!" Yara shouted, interrupting his thoughts. Peering through the mist, Tom saw that the still, dark water near the island swirled around into a murky funnel wide enough to swallow their boat. *She was right. We'll be sucked in!*

CREATURES OF THE DEEP

"Quick! Give me the oars!" Tom cried, leaping up to swap places with Elenna and Aroha. He quickly called on the magical strength of his golden breastplate. "Hold the rudder steady!" he told the others, rowing hard, his muscles straining against the deadly currents. Despite his efforts, the dark vortex of water drew closer. At its heart he saw a gaping emptiness.

The small boat started to tip to one side. Tom could feel the force of the whirlpool trembling through the wood beneath his feet. He gritted his teeth, making himself row even faster. His chest heaved as he struggled to steady their course. At the stern, Elenna and Aroha both had their hands on the tiller, bracing their weight against it as the current tried to wrench it from their grip.

Slowly, painfully, Tom managed to pull the vessel away from the swirling blackness, and out into still water. With the whirlpool a safe

distance away, he gave a sigh of relief. Elenna and Aroha slumped down on their bench. Beside them, Yara let out a shaky breath.

"That was close!" Tom said, wiping the sweat from his forehead.

Yara nodded. "I thought we were going—" She froze, her eyes widening as a tremor ran through the boat. Tom tensed, tightening his grip on the oars. Aroha frowned as another gentle bump rocked the vessel. Then another.

Tom leaned over, peering into the darkness, and gasped. A writhing mass of pale, giant eels swarmed below them, each with a gaping open jaw lined with jagged teeth.

"We have to get out of here.

Now!" Tom cried. One of the hideous things surged out of the water and fastened its jaw on to his oar. He slammed his oar against the side of the boat, smashing the creature off,

then started to row. Yara screamed. Elenna and Aroha leapt to their feet, making the boat rock wildly. "Look!" they cried, and pointed at the deck. Water was pouring into the dinghy from several holes as teeth like daggers chomped through the wood.

His heart thudding, Tom pulled faster and harder on the oars. Aroha drew her sword. Elenna snatched an arrow from her quiver, and each of them jabbed at the jaws that gnawed the wood. Water lapped at Tom's ankles, rising fast.

"We'll head for the next island," he cried. "We'll just have to hope there isn't a whirlpool there too!" Tom heaved on the oars, his muscles

burning. Elenna and Aroha stabbed
and slashed. Knee-deep in water,
even Yara had drawn her sword and
was thrusting at the wriggling eels.
But the boat was sinking.

"Abandon ship!" Tom cried. The
island was little more than a ridge
of rocks, but they had no choice.
When it was in reach, he got to his
feet and leapt out. The others all
sprang after him and clambered to
safety. Tom dragged the boat ashore,
using an oar to prise the remaining
creatures free. He joined the others,
breathing hard, as they stood on the
rocks, staring silently back at the
still, dark water.

Elenna shrugged. "What now?" she

asked. Tom peered across the lake,
through drifting banks of tattered
mist. The far shore of the mainland
was out there – somewhere. But
all he could make out were more

islands, poking from the water like broken teeth.

"Well, we can't go back into the lake," Yara said. "Think what those eels would do to our flesh!"

"We have no choice," Elenna said. "We can't stay here."

Tom thought of the way the pale eels had fixed on to his oar, and then on to the wood of the boat. "Maybe we can give the eels the slip," he suggested. "If we push the boat into the water on this side of the island, that gives us a chance to swim from the other side. The eels will be busy here."

Yara stared at Tom. "For all we know, the whole lake is filled with those things. And what about the Beast, Glaki?"

Aroha frowned. "It's risky," she said. "But I think we have to do as Tom says. Rotu needs us." She glanced towards the remains of their boat. "And there's no way back now, anyway."

"Before we go, you should remove your armour," Tom told Yara. "It will be almost impossible to swim in."

Yara shook her head. "A Royal Guard never removes her armour!"

Tom shrugged. Then, using an oar, he pushed what remained of the boat into the water. He gave it a mighty shove, launching it away from them. Almost at once, the water seemed to boil. A twisting mass of tangled, monstrous eels surrounded the vessel, their teeth splintering the wood. Tom turned away from the horrible sight and hurried to the far side of the island where the others had already walked over.

"Elenna and I will go first," Tom told the queen. "That way, if we are attacked, you and Yara might still make it with the jewels." He and Elenna looked down into the inky water.

"Ready?" Tom asked. Elenna had sworn she wouldn't swim in this lake, but now she nodded grimly. Tom took a deep breath, and together, they eased themselves carefully from the rocks.

Tom grimaced at the greasy, slimy touch of the water rising up his body as he waded deeper. When it reached his chest, he kicked out his legs and started to swim. He clenched his mouth firmly shut and raised his chin above the surface. Strange currents, some warm and others icy, tugged at his clothes. His flesh shrank away from them, and he shuddered, expecting at any moment to feel the bite of sharp teeth. Elenna stayed at his side, swimming grimly. They kept pushing through the brackish water until they were almost halfway to the next island.

"We're getting there," Tom gasped

to his friend.

"The sooner the better," Elenna said, above the smell.

Tom turned, treading water, and signalled for Aroha and Yara to follow.

As he started off again, he shivered, suddenly noticing how cold the water had become. He swam a few strokes, his arms and legs moving stiffly. The chill seemed to sap his strength. Elenna was slowing down too. Tom's teeth started to chatter, then his whole body began shaking. The touch of the water felt like icy needles jabbing his skin. He glanced back at Elenna to see her lips had turned blue.

"It's s-s-s-s-oooo c-c-c-cold,"
Elenna said. But just a short way
behind her, Yara and Aroha seemed
fine. They swam with strong, steady
strokes.

Slowly, Tom took his shield from his

back and pushed it towards Elenna.
"Take it!" he told her. "Nanook's
bell will warm you." Elenna gripped
the edge in one shaking hand and
started to paddle with the other, her
teeth clattering together. Tom could

feel his own limbs seizing up. His knees locked as he kicked, trying to keep afloat. He turned back towards the island to see a sheet of ice stretching towards him. What new danger was this? Only a moment ago, the water had been clear! Forcing his shuddering muscles to obey him, Tom reached the bank of ice. With numb fingers, he gripped the ice and heaved his sodden body out of the water. Lying flat on his belly, he turned. All he could see was thick, black ice. Aroha and Yara were still swimming towards him, but there was one figure missing from the lake.

Elenna had gone under.

FROZEN TO THE CORE

"Aroha! Yara!" Tom cried. "Elenna's trapped!" He fell to his hands and knees, peering into the water below, trying to catch sight of his friend. A moment later, Aroha and Yara were clambering up on to the shelf of ice.

"She'll drown!" Tom cried to Aroha, who immediately knelt beside him and pressed her face against the ice. "We have to find her!"

Yara stood shivering nearby, but before Tom could reprimand her, something pale appeared on the underside of the ice beneath where he knelt. *Elenna!* Tom slammed his fist down. Pain shot up his arm, but the ice didn't crack. He clambered to stand and stamped a foot on the ice instead, but only managed to chip the surface. Every second without air took Elenna a second closer to death! Panic rising in him, Tom drew his sword and hacked at the surface with the hilt, sending icy fragments flying. A crack shot through the thick ice. He smashed down with his sword hilt again and again, widening the crack, until he'd managed to make a hole.

"Help me!" he called to the queen, shoving his hand into the freezing water. His numb fingers met stiff

folds of fabric that were frozen solid. He clutched Elenna's collar. Aroha came beside him and grabbed her cloak. Together, they hauled Tom's best friend out on to the ice sheet. She lay there stiff and blue, her eyes frosted closed and Tom's shield still clutched between her hands.

She can't be dead. Tom knelt at her side, put his hands on his shield and called on the combined powers of Nanook's bell for warmth and Epos's talon for healing.

"Please work..." he muttered, staring intently at Elenna's still face while the magical tokens in his shield pulsed with heat beneath his palms. Nothing happened. A terrible pain clutched at Tom's heart. *Please...*

The frost covering Elenna's lashes turned to droplets of water. A flicker of hope stirred in Tom's chest as he saw his friend's cheeks turn from blue to white, then rosy pink. He leaned over her face and felt a faint breath.

"She's alive!" he cried.

"Tom! Quick!" Aroha shouted. "The ice is melting!" Tom tore his gaze from Elenna to see cracks appearing all around him, and water seeping up from below. Aroha grabbed Elenna's feet, as Tom gripped his friend under the shoulders. Together, they stumbled over the slippery, fractured surface. Tom lurched forwards, suddenly taking Elenna's full weight as Aroha let out a cry. The queen's foot had crashed through the ice, making her lose her balance. She managed to tug herself free, but all around them, the ice was breaking apart.

"Run!" Tom told Aroha. Calling on the magical strength of his breastplate, he hefted Elenna up over his shoulder and raced after the queen, leaping between floating chunks of ice, until he reached the solid rock of an island.

Finally, he set Elenna down on the shore, and bent over her. She had started to shiver, her colour returning to normal. Tom gently touched her shoulder, and she opened her eyes.

"What happened?" Elenna asked.

"The water turned to ice around you," Tom said. "You were frozen solid." Elenna sat up and frowned in confusion at the lake, still shuddering with cold. Not a single trace of the ice remained.

"But...how?" she managed.

Tom, Aroha and Yara all looked at each other. No one answered.

"We'll stop here awhile, so you can recover," Aroha said at last. "Then we must take our chance and swim for the next island."

While Elenna paced, rubbing the feeling back into her arms, Tom gazed around at the small island. Only twenty strides across at its widest point, the whole place was barren, apart from what looked like lumpy toadstools growing between the rocks.

Yara leaned down to inspect a clump of the fungus. "What ugly mushrooms," she said, poking at

the swollen grey flesh of one of the bulbous growths. *Poof!* The toadstool exploded, sending a puff of grey dust straight into Yara's face. She closed her eyes and let out a tremendous sneeze. *Poof!* Another mushroom burst open, then another in quick succession until the air was cloudy with spores. Tom coughed, waving the dust away, but it was hopeless. When the air finally cleared, they all had a dusting of grey spores over their hair and skin.

"Yuck!" Yara said. "Everything about this place is disgusting."

"At least the spores don't seem to be poisonous!" Tom said.

"Indeed," Aroha said. "Now, we

need to get going. We've wasted enough time here already." She turned to Elenna, who was still shivering slightly. "If you're ready, Elenna, that is?"

"Actually, I'm still warming up," Elenna said. "But if you're in such a hurry, please feel free to get going. And maybe you can take your useless bodyguard with you!"

Tom gaped at his friend and the queen. "Everyone," he said, "calm down, right now!"

Elenna and Aroha rounded on Tom at once. "Oh, shut up, Tom," they said.

"Hey!" Tom cried, hot blood rushing to his face. He turned to Elenna. "Don't you dare talk to me like that. Remember who just saved your life!"

"I didn't ask you to!" Elenna said, scowling. "I'm perfectly capable of looking after myself."

"Yeah, right," Yara scoffed. "You're about as much use in a crisis as a one-legged dog!"

Elenna let out a furious screech, snatching her bow from her back and aiming an arrow at Yara. "Say that again," Elenna growled. "I dare you."

"Don't worry, Yara," Aroha said, breezily. "Elenna couldn't hit a barn from two paces away! I don't know why we even bothered bringing Avantians on this Quest."

Hatred and fury burned inside Tom. He tore his sword from its sheath. "Don't try my patience, Your Majesty!" he snarled.

Aroha drew her own sword and lifted it high. "Or what?" she said, raising one eyebrow.

From the corner of his eye, Tom saw Yara tug her blade from her belt and start to circle Elenna.

"One more step…" Elenna warned, pulling her bow taut.

Then Aroha leapt towards Tom with a scream of rage, her sword slashing for his chest.

TOXIC RAGE

Tom lifted his shield to block the queen's strike. *SMASH!* The blow sent him reeling backwards. He caught his balance and lunged with his own blade at Aroha's smirking face. The queen ducked sideways, and his sword slashed through thin air.

Hearing a throaty screech, Tom

glanced across to see Elenna
wielding her bow like a club. She
smashed it across Yara's fingers,
knocking the sword from the
warrior's grip. Tom turned back
just in time to see Aroha barrelling

towards him.

Tom braced himself behind his shield. Aroha slammed into it, throwing him from his feet. He landed in the shallows of the lake, his face dipping below the water as the air was knocked from his lungs. Struggling up, gasping for breath, Tom shook the water away and his head seemed to clear. *What on earth am I doing?* Howls of fury filled his ears. He looked up to see Aroha marching towards him, her face contorted into a murderous scowl. Behind her on the island, Tom could see Yara on Elenna's back, trying to strangle her.

What's going on? Tom frowned,

taking in Aroha's bloodshot eyes, the grey spores covering her skin…

The toadstools!

Standing in the shallows, Tom sank into a crouch, his sword raised. Aroha let out a roar as she reached him, bringing her sword down in an arc towards his skull. Tom caught the blow on his own weapon. With their blades crossed, he reached out with his free hand and gripped the hilt of Aroha's sword. He twisted her arm and snatched the weapon from her grip. Aroha stumbled back, then came at him again, her face furious as she aimed a fierce punch. Tom ducked sideways to throw out his leg and sweep her feet from under her.

The queen sprawled forwards into the water. As soon as she was down, Tom landed on her back, shoving her face under the surface. Aroha thrashed wildly for a second before growing still. Tom let her go, and she stumbled up, wiping the water from her eyes. Then she frowned in confusion. From the island, Tom could hear grunts and growls as Yara and Elenna wrestled.

"What happened?" Aroha asked.

"It's the spores," Tom told Aroha. "They were making us crazed with anger. We must get Yara and Elenna into the water before they kill each other!" Aroha glanced past Tom at the fighting on the island and

winced. Tom turned to see Yara
holding Elenna by the hair. The
Tangalan warrior let out a grunt
and hurled Elenna on to the rocky
ground.

"Quickly!" Aroha said. Elenna

twisted on to her back, and Yara leapt towards her, stomping for her head. Handing Aroha her sword, Tom dived towards their two other companions. Elenna had managed to catch Yara's booted foot. She yanked it hard, sending the warrior sprawling. They both lay on the ground, catching their breath. Then they spied their fallen weapons and scrabbled for them.

"Stop!" Tom shouted, reaching the island as Yara and Elenna shot to their feet, armed once more. "It's the spores making you fight!"

"You've been poisoned!" Aroha told them from Tom's side. "Head for the water." Yara frowned at Tom for a moment. Elenna blinked at the queen. Then at the same moment, Elenna raised her bow like a cudgel and Yara brandished her sword. With deafening roars, they charged.

Tom managed to lift his blade just in time to parry Yara's blow, but the strength of it made him stagger. She swung for him again, in a two-handed swipe for his side. Tom caught her sword on his, deflecting the blow, then fell back a few paces, panting. Even in a fair fight, Yara would be a formidable opponent – but crazed with anger, she was terrifying. And Tom couldn't risk harming her. He heard a splash and glanced over to see Elenna rising from the water beside the queen, the murderous light gone from her eyes. *Thank goodness!*

"I could do with a hand over here!" Tom shouted as Yara lunged again, lifting her sword high in both hands. Tom blocked one mighty blow, then another, each sending pain jolting up his arm.

"Yara!" Aroha cried. The warrior spun towards her with a grunt. Elenna and Aroha stood side by side, Elenna holding her bow in her fist, and Aroha brandishing her sword. Yara hurtled towards them, her blade flashing through the air. Aroha swiped Yara's weapon aside, while Elenna smacked her bow across Yara's shins, sending her sprawling. Tom, Aroha and Elenna all pounced. Tom grabbed Yara's thrashing legs, while the others took her arms. Together, they heaved her towards the lake. As soon as they had Yara in the shallows, her frenzied movements slowed. Tom let go of her legs. Aroha and Elenna loosened their grip on her arms. Yara turned over, stumbled to her feet, then stood blinking at Tom, Elenna and Aroha.

"I... I'm so sorry..." Yara said at last. "I don't know what came over me."

"It was those toadstools and their spores," Aroha said. She looked at her feet. "I'm sorry too."

Elenna cleared her throat. "Well, we should get away from here, in case any more of those mushrooms explode," she said.

"Agreed," Tom said. "We still have Glaki to face. The last thing we need is to fight each other!"

The next island, a slender ridge of sharp rocks, was already in sight. Tom waded further into the murky lake, then started swimming. The others followed close behind him. As the water became deeper, Tom began to feel strange, chilly currents stirring all around him. Still, at least this time there weren't any eels or ice. Though his arms felt heavy and tired from fighting, he pushed himself to swim faster, his gaze fixed on the narrow strip of rock ahead. Suddenly, icy cold gripped hold of him, like an iron fist squeezing his body, making him gasp. He tried to cry out to warn the others but something in the depths coiled around his legs and pulled him down before he could even snatch a breath.

In the half-darkness of the silty lake, Tom found himself staring into the saucer-like purple eyes of a colossal eel. The creature's immense blue body looked bloated and dead as if rotting from within, the skin sloughing off in tatters. But his eyes were sharp and bright, alive with hatred and spite.

Glaki!

The Beast opened his giant
mouth, revealing long, needle-sharp
teeth that were as transparent as

shards of ice. Tom's heart clenched painfully. He couldn't feel his hands or feet, and a terrible, searing cold was spreading through his body, clutching hold of his lungs and his heart, freezing the blood in his veins.

He couldn't escape the Beast!

1

REVENGE

Suddenly, in a swirl of bubbles, Elenna appeared from above, clutching an arrow which she drove straight into Glaki's eye. The Beast writhed, letting go of Tom's legs, and dived lower, squirming in pain. Elenna grabbed Tom's arm and tugged him towards the surface. More hands gripped his body, and soon Aroha and Yara were helping Elenna pull him towards the island, then up on to the shelf of rock.

Clamping his teeth together against his shivering, Tom touched Nanook's bell in his shield, sighing with relief as warmth spread through his body.

"Are you all right?" Elenna asked.

Tom nodded. "Thanks to you," he said.

"Look!" Yara cried, pointing as Glaki's huge head, pockmarked and rotting, broke through the water of the lake, his long body rippling out behind it. One of the Beast's eyes had swollen shut, but the other watched them, gleaming with malice.

Through the power of the red
jewel in his belt, Tom heard Glaki's
voice in his mind: a hollow, rasping

hiss, like the wind through dead branches. *You can't stay there for ever*, Glaki told him. *Sooner or later, you will have to swim. And when you do. I will have you. No one enters my lake and lives!* The Beast sank back beneath the surface, leaving dark ripples in his wake.

"What now?" Yara asked. She turned to Aroha. "How far do you think we are from the other side of the lake?"

Aroha shrugged. "I don't know. None of these small islands are shown on the map. There's no way of telling." Looking out across the water, Tom could see no sign of solid ground – just more jutting rocks, shrouded in mist.

"I guess we have no option but to swim," Elenna said. "Maybe if we stay close together, we can fight if the Beast attacks?"

Tom shook his head. "Glaki almost killed me in seconds – he seems to be able to freeze people at will. We need to come up with a plan."

"I'm not sure we have time for that," Yara said, gazing back the way they had come. "Look."

Tom turned and saw something that made his mind reel. It looked like a torrent of rain, but instead of falling into the lake, the drops were rising up out of the water.

"Crystal arrows!" Elenna said.

Tom threw up his shield. "Get behind me," he told the others. Yara crouched at once. Elenna and Aroha soon followed suit. Tom angled his shield to catch the torrent of arrows whizzing towards them.

They arched high, then plunged all at once, hitting Tom's shield with the sound of shattering crystal. The volley of arrows struck with the force of steel, jolting his already aching arms.

"Ice!" Elenna said, picking up a glittering shard that instantly melted in her hand.

"I remember hearing that Glaki could create weapons from ice," Aroha said.

Tom tightened his grip on his shield and braced himself, while the others crouched behind him. Arrows battered Tom's shield and splintered down around them.

"Argh!" Aroha cried, and Tom

glanced around to see her clutching her shoulder, blood welling between her fingers. Rage flared in his chest.

"This is hopeless!" Tom cried. "I'm going out there to face him. Maybe I'll be enough of a distraction for you to all make it across the lake."

"How very noble of you," Yara said, rolling her eyes. "Although I suppose it's worth a try."

"No!" Elenna said, fiercely. "Glaki could freeze you in an instant. The water is his domain. You have no chance against him out there on your own."

But Elenna's words had given Tom an idea. "That's it!" he exclaimed, snapping his fingers. "We have to get Glaki out of the water."

"But how?" Aroha asked, frowning.

Tom and Elenna turned to each other with a grin. "A harpoon!" they both said at once. Tom drew his sword, and Elenna pulled their coil of rope from her pack.

"It's a shame it's not longer, but it'll have to do," Tom said, tying the rope firmly to the hilt of his sword. "Now, we'll just need to coax him closer."

Tom put his hand to the red jewel in his belt, ready to call to the Beast. But as he looked out at the lake, he saw the surface change, becoming as choppy as a sea during a storm.

"There's no wind or tide," Elenna

said, as waves started to crash against the island. "It must be the Beast doing this. Whoa!" Her face drained of colour. As Tom followed her gaze, he heard a roaring sound. He gulped as a colossal wave rose up, dwarfing the others, gaining height as it crashed towards them.

"Stand your ground!" Aroha shouted.

Tom braced himself, but he knew there was no way they could withstand the force of a tsunami. He gripped the hilt of his sword – their only hope against the Beast – and took a deep breath, hoping it wouldn't be his last.

7

HARPOON ATTACK

The terrific roar of the tidal wave filled Tom's ears as the mighty wall of water towered over them. *SWOOOSH!* Icy fists seemed to pummel Tom, battering his skull, snatching him from his feet. He pumped his arms and legs trying to right himself in the water, but

he didn't know which way was up. *CRACK!* His head hit rock with a sickening pain. Blood swirled and bubbles filled his vision. His lungs ached with lack of air. Finally, the water cleared a little, and Tom

could make out light streaming
down from above. He swam for the
surface, burst out into daylight and
took in gulping breaths of air.

He spotted Yara at once, bobbing
in the waves. Her face was pale, but

she looked uninjured.

"Tom!" Elenna called from behind him, and a moment later she was at his side. Glancing about, Tom saw Aroha surface. Her hair was plastered to her face.

"Head for the island!" the queen shouted, pointing towards the rocks just visible above the foaming tide. Then her eyes widened in shock, and with a sharp cry, she vanished beneath the waves.

"Aroha!" Yara cried, diving after her queen. Tom dived too, but couldn't see any trace of her, or the Beast. He surfaced quickly, just before Yara.

The Tangalan warrior shook her

head. "She's gone!" Yara said. "Glaki got her."

Anguish swelled inside Tom as he thought of his kind and noble queen, taken by a Beast. King Hugo was at home waiting for her, along with their baby son...

"No!" Tom roared, treading water. "I'm not leaving her to die!" He put his hand to the red jewel in his belt, and called out to the Beast.

"Coward!" Tom cried. "The woman you have captured is no Master of the Beasts! She has no magic, and no defence against evil like you! I am your enemy! I am the one you must defeat, and I demand you face me, worm!"

With a gurgling, bubbling sound, the water before Tom swelled, ballooning upwards, then fell away until he could see Aroha's body, blue-tinged and lifeless, lying in a coil of the Beast's decaying flesh. Glaki's head surged up from the

waves, and he glared down at Tom from a single cruel purple eye.

Come and get her! the Beast hissed in Tom's mind.

Elenna touched Tom's shoulder. She lifted the soaked, frayed end of the rope from the water, still connected to his sword, then dipped her head towards the island just behind them. "This is our chance," she said. "I'll secure this to a rock."

Tom nodded as he understood Elenna's plan. "Time to go fishing," he said.

Striking off towards the Beast, Tom swam with long, powerful strokes. Before he could reach the putrid coils of flesh that held the queen, Glaki disappeared beneath the surface, taking Aroha with him. Through the magic of the red jewel in his belt, Tom could hear Glaki's taunting, hissing laughter. The Beast had not gone far.

Tom swam a few more strokes, drawing his sword from its scabbard with one hand, then stopped, treading water. He felt a faint current stir around him, and braced himself. *WHOOSH!* A mighty spout of water burst upwards, making Tom's stomach swoop as it lifted him up. As the torrent carried him higher, he caught sight of the Beast's bloated, tattered coils and let his harpoon fly.

Yes! Tom's sword bit deep into the Beast's pale flesh. Black blood oozed out, billowing into the water.

A shudder of pain ran through Glaki's coils before he darted downwards, heading for the depths. Tom felt himself suddenly falling, his stomach dropping away with the water, until he was sucked under in the Beast's wake. But before he could do anything, he was spat out again by the churning waves, narrowly missing being smashed against the island's jagged shore.

"Tom!" Elenna cried from the shelf of rock. "Help!" She and Yara had hold of the rope and were hauling on it, dragging Glaki's massive body through the water. Tom heaved himself on to the island and rushed to join them. With the three of them pulling together, tugging with all their strength, Glaki's writhing form edged slowly but surely out of the water and on to the rocks.

Finally, Glaki lay squirming on dry land, black blood seeping from where Tom's sword had pierced his flesh. His single eye was rolling in agony. The Beast looked somehow smaller, almost pitiful. Tom didn't feel any sympathy, but also, he didn't feel a single thrill of victory – because there, held tightly in a coil of the Beast's body, Aroha lay motionless. Her eyes were closed and her skin was deathly white.

TRAITORS TO THE CROWN

The Beast gave one final shudder and then fell still, his body slack and his one remaining eye a hideous milky white. Tom and Elenna rushed to Aroha. Each of them gripped one of her shoulders, and tugged her lifeless body from Glaki's loosened coils. Her flesh felt

cool to the touch – but not ice cold,
which gave Tom hope. When he bent
low over her body, though, he could
tell that she wasn't breathing. *No!
She can't be gone...* He felt a shove,
and Yara pushed past him. She
bent and started tugging at Aroha's

clothes. *Yara's right*, Tom thought, hope kindling inside him. *There's still a chance to revive her!* Tom stepped back, giving the warrior space to work.

"Got them!" Yara said, pulling the pouch containing the Jewels of

Tangala from inside Aroha's tunic.

Tom and Elenna stared at her. "What are you doing?" Tom asked, not able to believe what he was seeing.

"We owe it to Aroha to continue the mission," Yara said. "We need the jewels to rescue her nephew!"

With a growl of disgust, Elenna stalked past Yara and then knelt beside the queen. She tipped her head back. Then, gently opening Aroha's mouth and pinching her nose, Elenna breathed into the queen's lungs. Tom dropped to Aroha's other side and started chest compressions. They worked together in silence. After a short while, he and Elenna sat back to study the queen's still face. Nothing. Not the faintest flicker of life. Tom tried to swallow the terrible ache in his throat. *How can I return to King Hugo and tell him she's gone?*

"I'm not giving up!" Elenna said, fiercely. She lowered her lips to the queen's once more. Tom clasped his hands, one on top of the other. He laid them on Aroha's chest...

...and felt a spasm of movement!

Elenna sat up sharply. Aroha's hands flailed as she struggled to rise. Her eyes flickered open, staring in panic as she choked. Giddy with relief, Tom propped Aroha up, slapping her back. She gasped and

coughed, spewing up water.

Once her breathing had returned
to normal, Aroha pointed towards
Glaki's body. "The Beast!" she croaked.
"He's defeated." She rummaged inside
her tunic but brought her hand out

empty. "Where are the jewels?"
Aroha asked, frowning.

Tom and Elenna shared a glance
as Yara quickly stepped forward,
holding the small bag.

"Here, Your Majesty!" she said,
handing it to the queen with a low
bow. Aroha frowned, as though
wondering how the pouch had
worked its way out of her tunic.
Then she took the pouch. Tom saw
an ice-blue light shining through
the canvas. Reaching into her bag,
Aroha pulled out the gem and held
it up.

Tom gasped as a thousand tiny
points of light scattered over the
Beast's massive body. Beneath them,

Glaki's flesh transformed from its mottled blue to a transparent crystal shade, and in an instant it melted away altogether. The glittering lights swarmed together like fireflies, then streamed back into the gem in Aroha's hand, which pulsed brightly for an instant and went dark.

"We did it!" Yara cried, punching the air. "Come, Aroha, we have only one more Beast to fight before we can free your nephew!" She held out a hand to the queen.

"No!" Elenna cried, stepping between them. "Aroha, you can't trust her. Just a moment ago, Yara was about to leave you for dead. She

took the jewels from your lifeless
body — they are the only things she
cares about!"

Aroha staggered to her feet, then
drew herself up to her full height.
"I know who I can trust, and who
I can't," she said. "Get out of my
way!"

Elenna didn't budge. Tom stepped
to her side. "Elenna's right," Tom
told the queen. "Yara's been acting
strangely the whole time we've
been on this Quest. I wouldn't be
surprised if she's worked with
Zargon since the start. What if she
let him kidnap Rotu just to get you
to bring him the jewels?"

"Don't be ridiculous!" Aroha

said, her eyes flashing with anger. "Kneel before me now, the pair of you!" Tom dropped to his knees, his cheeks stinging as if he'd been slapped. After a moment's hesitation, Elenna did the same.

"I know who is a traitor to the crown and who is not!" Aroha said. She closed her eyes, gathering herself for a moment, as if too furious to continue. "Yara is like family to me, and you have questioned her motives from the start," she said at last. "I will not stand for it any longer. You have let me down again and again on this Quest. I should never have let you come in the first place!"

"But we just saved your life!" Elenna protested.

"And I would expect nothing less from any of my subjects," Aroha said. "But with the safety of Tangala and Avantia at stake, I require absolute loyalty. I cannot have you questioning my judgement or making accusations against my nephew's bodyguard. It is not your place to argue with your queen."

As Tom struggled to make sense of what he was hearing, the sun suddenly brightened, causing him to blink and refocus his eyes. The mist hanging above the water quickly burned away, and the water cleared until Tom could see glittering white sand beneath it, scattered with pink shells. And, with the mist gone, Tom could see the far shore of the lake.

"Aroha!" Yara cried. "Look! We're almost across! And the water looks shallow enough to wade through."

The queen glanced over her

shoulder. "We shall set off at once!"
she told Yara, then turned back to
Tom and Elenna.

"Go home to Avantia," she told
them coldly. "Yara and I will
complete this Quest alone." Aroha
turned and stalked away from Tom
and Elenna, joining Yara. Together,
they waded into the sparkling water
of the Crystal Sea.

Tom got to his feet, and so did
Elenna. They stood together,
frowning after the queen.

"What was that all about?"
Elenna asked. "Do you think the
spores from those mushrooms are
still making her unable to think
straight? Or did she hit her head

when Glaki pulled her under?"

"I don't know," Tom said, feeling heavy with dread. "But something's not right. It makes no sense for Aroha to trust Yara over us. One thing's for certain, though. I'm not turning back. I promised King Hugo I would keep Aroha safe. And while there's blood in my veins, I shall!"

THE END

CONGRATULATIONS, YOU HAVE COMPLETED THIS QUEST!

At the end of each chapter you were awarded a special gold coin. The QUEST in this book was worth an amazing 8 coins.

Look at the Beast Quest totem picture opposite to see how far you've come in your journey to become

MASTER OF THE BEASTS.

The more books you read, the more coins you will collect!

Do you want your own Beast Quest Totem?

1. Cut out and collect the coin below
2. Go to the Beast Quest website
3. Download and print out your totem
4. Add your coin to the totem

www.beastquest.co.uk

READ THE BOOKS, COLLECT THE COINS!
EARN COINS FOR EVERY CHAPTER YOU READ!

550+ COINS
MASTER OF THE BEASTS

410 COINS
HERO →

350 COINS
WARRIOR

230 COINS
KNIGHT →

180 COINS
SQUIRE

44 COINS
PAGE →

8 COINS
APPRENTICE

550+
515
480
445
410
395
380
365
350
320
290
260
230
217
206
191
180
146
112
78
44
30
19
8

READ ALL THE BOOKS IN SERIES 25:
THE PRISON KINGDOM!

AKORTA
THE ALL-SEEING APE

LYCAXA
HUNTER OF THE PEAKS

GLAKI
SPEAR OF THE DEPTHS

DIPROX
THE BUZZING TERROR

Don't miss the next exciting Beast Quest book: DIPROX, THE BUZZING TERROR!

Read on for a sneak peek...

OUTCASTS

Tom waded out of the cool, clear water of the Crystal Sea and up on to its shingle beach. His boots squelched and his jerkin clung to his skin. Beside him, Elenna shook a rain of glittering droplets from her hair.

She glanced around. "I can't see any sign of Yara or the queen," Elenna said, her voice tight with worry.

Tom shaded his eyes against the sun, searching the bleak landscape ahead. Beneath the deep blue sky, mounds of pebbles stretched into the distance. Apart from the gentle lapping of waves, there was no other sound.

Tom sighed. "They can't be that far ahead of us."

"At least we know where they're going," Elenna said.

Tom nodded, remembering how the Crystal Sea formed a ring around the island. "Zargon's palace must be straight on. Let's go."

After filling their water bottles, they set off, jogging over the shingle beach. Tom kept his eyes on the horizon, watching for any sign of Queen Aroha, or a Beast. Since they had arrived in Zargon's enchanted Kingdom of Vakunda in search of the queen's kidnapped nephew, they had already defeated three fearsome enemies. Tom knew one final Beast still awaited them, along with the Evil Wizard Zargon himself. Worry gnawed at his gut. He hated to think of Aroha facing such deadly foes without him and Elenna.

"I still can't understand why the queen would take Yara's side against us," he said. "It makes no sense – we've risked our lives again and again on this Quest. All Yara's done is get in the way, or worse. Aroha's no fool. What's got into her?"

"Perhaps she's still affected by those poisonous fungi that made us all fight each other," said Elenna. "Or maybe she can't believe that someone who has guarded her nephew for so long would betray her."

Tom remembered the look of fury on the queen's face when she ordered him and Elenna to abandon the Quest. "Either way," he said, "it's still down to us to protect her, and the jewels."

Zargon had demanded the Jewels of Tangala as a ransom for the prince. Even before Tom had seen the power of the gemstones at work, he knew that letting them fall into the wrong hands would be disastrous. Seeing how they could absorb the energy of defeated Beasts, and transform entire landscapes for the better, he was more determined than ever to keep them safe.

They reached the top of a crest in the land, and Tom saw that the shingle beach gave way to sand dunes baking under the sun. Elenna pointed to two sets of footprints leading into the distance, and they set off, jogging as fast as they

could; but the powdery sand shifted
with every step, making running
exhausting. The sun blazed down,
and Tom soon felt parched, but he
forced himself onwards. Each time
he reached the top of a new dune, he
hoped to catch sight of Aroha, or of

Zargon's palace, but all there was to
see was the barren sand stretching
on and on, shimmering in a dazzling
heat haze.

Finally, dizzy with thirst, Tom drew
to a halt before a wide, flat stretch of
desert. "Surely we have to be close to

catching them," he panted.

"I hope so!" Elenna said, leaning her hands on her knees to get her breath. After taking a long drink of water, Tom called on the power of his enchanted helmet, part of his Golden Armour. The full suit was back in Avantia, but Tom was still able to draw on its magic to allow him to see across great distances. He could just make out two tiny figures. Beyond them, there was a line of something that glittered even more than the desert mirages.

"They're still a long way off!" Tom told Elenna.

"Then we'd better keep going," Elenna said, grimly. The sun climbed higher as they ran, the only sound the rasp of their breath in the hot, dry air. Tom's throat felt raw and his chapped lips were cracked and bleeding. But he could see the queen's glinting form, gradually drawing closer. *We're gaining on them!*

Read
DIPROX, THE BUZZING TERROR
to find out what happens next!

Beast Quest
ULTIMATE HEROES

Find out more about
the NEW mobile game at
www.beast-quest.com

GET IT ON
Google Play

Download on the
App Store

*et three new heroes with
power to tame the Beasts!*